D1631181

Scaredy Cat

First published in Great Britain 1985 by Heinemann Young Books
an imprint of Reed International Books Limited.
Michelin House, 81 Fulham Rd, London SW3 6RB
Mammoth paperback edition first published 1998
Published in hardback by Heinemann Educational Publishers,
a division of Reed Educational and Professional Publishing Limited
by arrangement with Reed International Books Limited.
Text copyright © Anne Fine 1985
Illustrations copyright © Nick Ward 1998
The Author and Illustrator have asserted their moral rights
Paperback ISBN 0 7497 3375 6
Hardback ISBN 0 434 80295 6
10 9 8 7 6 5 4 3 2 1
A CIP catalogue record for this title is available from the British Library
Printed at Oriental Press Limited, Dubai

ANNE FINE

Scaredy Cat

Illustrated by
Nick Ward

 **YELLOW BANANAS**

For Cordelia

Chapter One

THE SKIPPING ROPE whipped round and round. Everyone was singing:

'Cinderella,

Dressed in yellow,

Went up town to meet a fellow.

On the way

Her girdle busted.

How many people

Were disgusted?

One, two, three, four . . .'

Poppy jumped as high and as rhythmically as she could. She was a good skipper, and she was out to beat her own record.

1

'Eleven, twelve, thirteen . . .'

Martha and Kate, turning the rope, were the only two still counting aloud. Poppy was saving her breath now. Out of the corner of her eye she could see all the others standing in a group beside the school wall, waiting for their turns inside the rope. They were whispering to one another.

'Poppy doesn't want to go!'

'Twenty-two, twenty-three . . .'

'Where?'

'Over to the Big School tomorrow. To the Horror Show.'

'Why not?'

'She's afraid.'

'She says she doesn't like things like that.'

'Thirty-four, thirty-five . . .'

'Poppy's a chicken.'

'A scaredy-cat! A scaredy-cat!'

Poppy could hear them talking about her above the scrunch of her shoes on the hard ground, though she kept a brave face and pretended she couldn't, and Kate counted loudly, trying to drown the ·chatter out. She was a good friend.

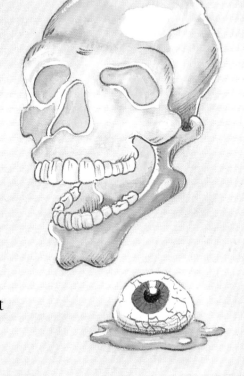

'Forty-one, forty-two . . .'

'What's she scared of? The way they make the room completely dark?'

'The eyes that light up green inside the skeleton's skull?'

'The horrid messes they make you stick your fingers in, and tell you that they're pirates' eyeballs?'

'The creepy noises? All those groans and shrieks?'

'Everyone likes the Big School Horror Show!'

'Poppy doesn't. She says she hates things like that.'

'Fifty-six, fifty-seven . . .'

'Scaredy-cat!'

Poppy could feel her face reddening. She hoped that everyone would think it was because of the skipping, which was going faster and faster as Martha speeded up, trying to get Poppy out so her own turn would come round again.

'Sixty-one, sixty-two . . .'

'She'll have to go. The whole class is going. It's been arranged.'

'Maybe she'll cry.'

'Or scream.'

'Or faint.'

'Or go blue in the face.'

'Or froth at the mouth.'

Everyone burst out laughing. It was too much. Although she was within sight of her record, eighty-one, Poppy pretended the rope

5

had tripped her. She kept her feet down on the ground whilst it grazed through the air towards her bare leg, and slapped down hard on it, hurting her badly. Tears pricked behind her eyes, but before any of the rest of them could catch her crying she pulled her foot free from the rope's tangle and ran off, without a word, to the other side of the playground.

'Hey! That's not fair!'
'Poppy! It's your turn to take the end of the rope. Come back!'

Poppy pretended that she couldn't hear them above the hubbub in the playground. She raced around the side of the building straight into the caretaker, who had been strolling peaceably across the tarmac, swinging a bucket.

'Whoops!'

'Ouch!'

It was a fast and hard collision and Poppy crumpled into a puddle, in tears. The caretaker put down his bucket, reached for her and lifted her to her feet. He brushed the worst wet off her jacket and then took a rather grubby handkerchief from his trouser pocket and wiped the tear stains from her cheeks. Poppy looked round to see if anyone was watching; but there were only a few of the little ones from the nursery close by, and they didn't count. Nobody minded being caught crying by them.

The caretaker rubbed his damaged knee.

'Crippled, I shouldn't wonder,' he said. 'Possibly for life. Which one are you?'

'I'm Poppy,' Poppy said.

'Poppy,' he said. 'Right-ho. I shall remember you, Poppy. And if I didn't have a bell to ring, I'd stop and have a little chat with you about Playground Safety and Keeping Death Off The Tarmac.'

'I'm sorry about
your knee,' Poppy told him.
   'That's very civil of you,'
the caretaker said. 'Considering . . .'
And picking up his bucket, he
began limping heavily across the
playground towards the back door. It took
Poppy some moments to convince herself that
he was only putting it on, and by that time
the bell had stopped ringing and it was time
to hurry back inside.

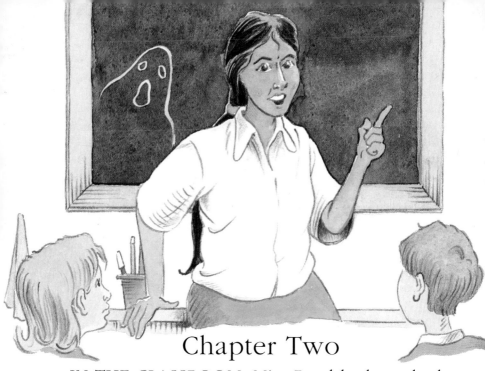

Chapter Two

IN THE CLASSROOM, Miss Patel had perched
on the edge of her desk and embarked upon
one of her speeches.

'Chairs straight,' she called. 'Arms folded.
Mouths buttoned up. That means you, too,
Charles. Henry, take your feet off the back of
Alicia's chair. Alicia, stop sniggering. Be quiet,
all of you, and listen.'

Poppy settled more comfortably on her
wooden chair and stared through the layers of
grime on the window pane out into the
playground. She considered herself most

fortunate to have the only place in the
classroom from which one could stare out of
the window and yet not appear to Miss Patel
to be doing so. Poppy didn't, like Kiva, have
to turn her head. She didn't, like Arif, have to
crane her neck round her neighbour to get a
view. She could just slide her eyes slightly
towards the left and watch whatever was
happening out there, like the caretaker
sweeping up the leaves around the huge oak
tree that stood in the middle of the
playground, or the fathers and mothers and
babysitters gathering at the gates
just before noon, waiting for
their children to emerge
from the nursery.

   She could watch babies
bellowing red-faced in
their prams and push-chairs,
disobedient puppies

leaping about at the ends of their leads, and giant flowery umbrellas whipping inside out whenever the wind was fierce. Miss Patel was never the wiser, unless Poppy forgot to make the occasional scratching on her workbook with her pencil, or forgot to turn the page of her reading book from time to time, or let the expression on her face slip from one of meek concentration to one of blank daydreaming.

For Poppy was a daydreamer. Whenever she

found it hard to think of anything to write in her Daily Diary, whenever the answer to seven times eight, or nine times seven, escaped her, Poppy stared out of the window. If Miss Patel embarked upon one of her great long speeches, Poppy at once became distracted by anything happening out in the playground, or, if it was totally deserted, by nothing at all but her own thoughts.

Today, though, she didn't have to look far for something to distract her. The caretaker was sitting on his heels right under her window, patching up all the places on the sill where the paint had flaked away. He was so close that she could see the bright fresh green paint flecks on his brown hair, and the gaps between his teeth whenever he left his mouth open, concentrating on a tricky corner. He'd opened the window a little, to dab his brush as far back as the window frame, and she could even hear him humming under his breath. And just as she could hear him, he could hear what was being said inside. He was so startled he nearly upset his paint can when, without warning, Miss Patel called out:

'Poppy! Young lady, are you listening to me?'

Poppy drew her attention back smartly.

Miss Patel continued:

'The Big School Horror Show is now arranged for tomorrow afternoon. I know how much you all enjoyed it last year.'

Poppy shuddered. 'I know

how much you're all looking forward to going again.' Poppy scowled. 'But I am warning you . . .' Poppy looked up, hopefully. 'One spark of trouble, one spot of misbehaviour . . .' The rest of the class waited, chairs straight, arms folded, mouths buttoned up, for the appalling, unthinkable threat: 'One mite of naughtiness, from anyone, and you shan't go, none of you, not one, *nobody*.'

Nobody spoke. Nobody stirred. Miss Patel folded her arms and said in the most dreadful tones: 'Unless whoever is the cause of the trouble goes straight over to the Big School and explains to Miss Heap in person exactly what they have done and how sorry they are.'

A ripple of shock ran round the classroom. Eyes widened. Friends gaped at one another. Explain? To Miss Heap? Why, even the tallest children from the Big School melted away when she came round a corner. Whole gangs moved to the other side of the playing field if she drew near. Silence fell down the whole length of a corridor if her shadow so much as

15

fell through an open doorway.

Miss Heap was no ordinary person to whom one could, if hard pressed, try and explain things. She was tall and menacing, chilling and terrifying. At her approach the very bravest quaked. Explain to Miss Heap? Just the idea was sufficiently alarming to keep Henry's feet off the back of Alicia's chair until the very last afternoon of the term.

And Miss Patel knew it. She beamed at them. 'Shall we get on?' she asked sweetly. 'How about some nice long division?'

As all the work cards were

16

shared out, and pencils sharpened, Poppy stared out of the window and brooded.

Her main hope, a very private hope that she would not even have shared with Kate, was that someone in the class, anyone, might behave badly. There was, she thought, hope. Only the week before, Katherine had got into terrible trouble for putting four spiders on the peanut butter in her sandwich and eating it in front of the horrified nursery children. And what about that great row the morning Arif walked past the lollipop man at the school gate with two worms dangling from his mouth, claiming that he was Dracula's nephew? And then there was the riot the day Miss Patel was called to the telephone and the class was left alone for twenty minutes with the percussion instruments. Surely something like that might happen before tomorrow afternoon? Something half as bad? A quarter, even?

But, looking about her, Poppy could see

that there was really very little chance. The classroom was unusually quiet. Even Henry sat with his legs clamped firmly under his own chair, sucking his pencil and staring at his long division work card as fixedly as if it were a cartoon book. No, no hope there. Clearly everyone was desperate to get to the Big School Horror Show. Everyone except Poppy.

E HORROR SH
IS COMING...
BE THERE!

Chapter Three

WAS POPPY A scaredy-cat? She'd certainly
never thought of herself that way. She had
been brave enough when the doctor put five
stitches in her foot after she stepped on
broken glass at the beach. She had been
brave enough to chase that fierce dog away
from Kate's kitten. If Poppy could only see
the thing she feared, be quite sure exactly
what it was, then she could face it. But switch
television channels to a creepy film, and
Poppy would be out of the room in an instant.

And when Kate's father told a bedtime ghost

story, it was no good: however much Poppy
had been looking forward to sleeping over at
Kate's house, she'd have to be wrapped in a
blanket and carried home in her nightie,
however late it was.

Was she a scaredy-cat? She simply hated the
Horror Show, when pupils from the Big
School banded together to put on the
spookiest show they could imagine in the

darkest part of the basement. They all dressed up as ghosts and demons and monsters. There was always a Dracula whose teeth dripped blood and a Frankenstein's monster with a rusty bolt through his neck. The music was eerie and the words of the songs so creepy that they echoed in Poppy's ears for days after.

The show ran all day, and every class in turn was invited. Everyone loved it and begged for the chance to be one of the chosen few to be invited onto the stage and frightened out of their wits in the haunted

dungeon sketch, or the graveyard scene.

Everyone except Poppy. She loathed every minute. Last year she'd come out of the show as pale as a maggot. All the rest laughed and joked on their way back up the steps into the daylight. When they saw Poppy's face they had all shouted: 'Look, Miss Patel, Poppy's going to faint.'

'There was no air down there,' Miss Patel had said. But Poppy knew better.

She could, she thought, go up and ask Miss Patel to let her off going. Maybe she could stay behind and tidy the bookshelves, or something. But when Martha asked to be allowed off singing because of her sore throat, Miss Patel had only answered: 'Just go and croak, dear, like all the others.'

And when Misao deliberately forgot to bring her swimsuit, so she would not have to go swimming, Miss Patel led her down the steps at the shallow end, wearing only her stripy vest and her panties. No hope there, either.

It was, Poppy saw, at least as hard a

problem as any
on the long division card.
And though she worked at both in turn for
the rest of the morning, she was no nearer a
solution to either when the caretaker walked
across the playground to ring the lunch bell.
Poppy watched through the grey window as
he ambled around the tree towards her.

Noticing the look of sheer despair on her face, the caretaker broke into a terrible limp to try and cheer her. But Poppy could not even smile.

Lunch was a miserable affair. Poppy could swallow scarcely a mouthful for worrying. Not only that, but everyone at the table seemed to be getting into a Big School Horror Show mood.

'A dead pirate's eye!' shrieked Lisa, prodding Poppy's hard-boiled egg with her inky finger.

'Blood bun!' cried Kevin, biting into the salmon paste spread on his bread.

Even Kate stuck her finger into Poppy's milk and said: 'Watered down dried bones. Oh, I can't wait until tomorrow!'

Poppy simply hung down her head and said nothing.

The afternoon seemed to pass slower than any Poppy ever remembered. Everyone was behaving perfectly. The class was going over the names of shapes. Miss Patel called the children, one by one, up to the blackboard and handed over the chalk.

'Draw me a hexagon, Misao,' she'd say. 'Elizabeth, draw me a rhombus. Now, George, you do a polygon. Arif, I want a pyramid from you.' Poppy stared out of the window, far too anxious to pay attention, until her name was called.

'Poppy. Poppy! What are you daydreaming about now? Wake up and come and draw a rectangle.'

Poppy scraped back her chair and tore her eyes unwillingly away from the window. She made her way between the tables. As she took the chalk from Miss Patel, she did her very best to concentrate.

But suddenly the only shape in her mind was that fat, oval, hard-boiled egg in her lunch box that Lisa had prodded with her finger. It filled her mind so completely that when she stood in front of the blackboard, she quite forgot what she'd been asked to draw on it. The chalk squeaked as she pressed hard to get a strong white line. And while the

class sat perfectly still and silent, Poppy drew
her shape.

As soon as she had finished, she stepped back. Only then did she notice, to her shame and horror, that she had drawn, not a rectangle at all, but an oval. Staring at Poppy from the blackboard was a fat, white, dead pirate's eye!

The class began to whisper.

'Poppy did that on purpose!'

'Everyone knows how to draw a rectangle. Even Poppy!'

'The scaredy-cat's trying to stop us from going.'

Even her friend Kate stared at her reproachfully from her seat in the front row, and said, 'Poppy!'

The whole class was glaring at her. Poppy was horrified. Her eyes filled with tears and the chalk slipped from her fingers. She didn't wait for Miss Patel to speak. She didn't wait to hear more of the furious whispers. Before Miss Patel could put out a hand to prevent her, she ran to the door, wrenched it open, and fled. She clattered down the staircase, through the swing doors and into the nursery cloakroom where no one would think of looking for her, and only the little ones might catch her crying.

Poppy crouched down beside the radiator and, burying her head in her arms, she sobbed and sobbed. Never in her whole life had she felt so trapped and miserable.

Chapter Four

AND IT WAS here that the caretaker came across her a few minutes later, her face as wet as if she'd been walking in a thunderstorm, her sleeves quite sodden from mopping at the tears that kept falling.

'Poppy!' he said, shutting the door quietly behind him. 'Oh, I remember you. I said I would.'

He reached down to help her to her feet. Drawing the same grubby handkerchief as before from his trouser pocket, he dabbed and blotted the tears on her face.

'Getting to be a bit of a habit, this,' he remarked. 'Practically old friends now, aren't we?'

Poppy couldn't speak for swallowing, so she just nodded obediently.

'Right,' said the caretaker. 'Old friends. And friends share their problems, don't they?'

Poppy shook her head. She didn't want to share this problem, not with anyone. But the caretaker didn't seem to notice.

'Right,' he said again. 'So what's the problem? You can tell me.'

'I can't,' said Poppy. 'It's too awful.'

'Too awful?' said the caretaker, staring. 'Too *awful?* Have you strangled your grandmother with your skipping rope?'

'No,' hiccupped Poppy.

'Have you roasted the next door baby in a hot oven, for supper?'

'No,' Poppy said.

'Have you stolen my bucket, or rung my bell without permission?'

'No,' Poppy assured him.

'Then,' said the caretaker, 'it's not too awful. Worse things are happening all the time, everywhere. Why, only across the playground, in the Big School, a woman called Miss Heap is close to throwing herself into the river to drown because she's done something *far* more awful.'

'What?'

'She's lost a pupil! That's all! Can you imagine? Someone from this part of the school, no older or taller than you, I expect. Lost. Gone. Fled. Run away from the classroom! Miss Heap is quite beside herself. She's half demented with grief and worry. Chewing her fingernails, fretting horribly. Fancy the shame of it! To be headmistress of a school and lose a child! She'll lose her job, too, I shouldn't wonder, if this particular child doesn't turn up again, go along to the Big School and explain, and set Miss Heap's poor mind at rest again.'

'No!' Poppy said.

'Oh, yes,' the caretaker insisted. 'Otherwise

heaven only knows what will happen.'

He paused, his face stricken, as though he could see perfectly plainly in his mind's eye Miss Heap's corpse floating steadily down the river into which she'd thrown herself, half mad with grief and worry.

'Oh, dear,' said Poppy.

'I'll tell you what,' the caretaker said. 'You're not busy, are you? I mean, here you are, taking a nice little nap beside this warm radiator. Would you mind doing me a bit of a favour? Walk across with me to Miss Heap's office . . .'

Poppy tried to pull her hand free, but the caretaker was holding her fingers a little too firmly in his own.

'Just in case . . .'

'Just in case?'

'Just in case you should bump into this other little girl who's run away. Just in case she decides to come back and explain what happened, so poor Miss Heap won't throw herself in the river. Just in case this little girl doesn't know where Miss Heap's office is. If I show you, then you can show her. If she comes back . . .'

Poppy was silent for a few moments.

'All right,' she said at last. 'But just in case.'

Chapter Five

LOOKING BACK ON it later, Poppy could never quite make out just how it was that the caretaker disappeared down the corridor so silently and so quickly, the moment the door to Miss Heap's office opened. And come to that, she wasn't sure whether that bang he made on the door with his bucket a moment before was quite the accident he later claimed. It was a hard enough bang. It certainly brought Miss Heap to the door promptly enough.

Another strange thing: Miss Heap hadn't much of the look of someone half mad with grief and worry. Busy? Yes, certainly. Impatient? Very. But close to throwing herself in the river? Hardly. Even Poppy could tell she was barely bothering to listen to the slow, faltering explanation.

'What?' she kept saying. 'Yes, yes. Get on. But what's the *problem?*'

So, in the end, Poppy just came out with it. Just like that. And just like chasing away the dog that went after Kate's kitten, and counting the stitches being put in her foot along with the doctor, it wasn't so bad. Nowhere near so bad as dead pirates' eyes, and glowing eyes in the darkness, and horrible noises.

'Please,' she said. 'Please, Miss Heap. I don't want to go to the Horror Show with all the others tomorrow. I hate Horror Shows. I can't sleep after them, and, if I do, they give me nightmares.'

There. It was done. She had said it.

And nothing terrible happened. Only Miss Heap looking down at Poppy more closely through narrowed eyes.

'Mmmm,' Miss Heap said, after a moment's reflection. 'I don't suppose that Miss Patel has sent you all the way over here to see me personally, for nothing. Tell me, which one are you?'

'I'm Poppy,' said Poppy.

'Poppy,' she said. 'Poppy, wait here for just a moment while I write a note for you to take back to your classroom.'

The note she handed Poppy a minute later was neatly folded into quarters. Halfway down a deserted corridor on the way back, Poppy unfolded it carefully. It said:

Poppy read the note through. Then she folded it very neatly into quarters again, and smiled to herself.

When she walked through the classroom door, every head lifted to stare at her. Everyone watched as she walked across to Miss Patel and handed her the note. Everyone watched as Miss Patel read it and smiled, and put it away inside the register. Everyone watched Miss Patel pat Poppy on the back, and the ones at the front, like Kate, even heard Miss Patel saying to Poppy:

'There! That was very brave of you, I must say. I thought for a moment, when you rushed out, that you'd run off somewhere to hide, all frightened and upset. But then the caretaker came in to tell me you'd gone straight off to talk to Miss Heap.'

39

Kate said, 'Is it all right again? Are we going?'

'You're going,' Miss Patel assured them all. 'Thanks to Poppy.'

There was another sudden burst of whispering. Her cheeks glowing, Poppy heard everything they were saying about her. And there was not one mention, this time, of scaredy-cats.

The next day, while everyone else was away at the Big School Horror Show, Poppy sat happily tidying the bookshelves. Suddenly behind her there was an unfamiliar rubbing and squeaking noise. Poppy looked round. There, at the window, was the caretaker. He had a wet cloth in his hand and was polishing the panes till they sparkled.

Poppy went over and unlatched the window.

'Hello.'

'Hello, Poppy. Miss Patel asked me to keep an eye on you while everyone's away. So here I am, cleaning your window, brightening your life.'

'Thank you,' said Poppy. 'Thank you very much. For everything.'

The caretaker winked at her.

'Don't mention it,' he said. 'It was nothing. Considering . . .'

He beamed at Poppy through the gleaming window pane, and Poppy beamed back.